The Wolf Who Ate the Sky

Mary Daniel Hobson and Anna Isabel Rauh
Images and design by Charles Hobson

Heyday, Berkeley, California

Once upon a time there was a wolf who was so hungry that when he went to bed he said, "When I wake up, I am going to eat the first thing I see."

The next morning when he opened his eyes, the first thing he saw was the sky.

So he opened his mouth wide and in one big gulp swallowed the whole sky.

And the world went dark.

There was no place for the sun to shine,
and no place for the clouds to dance,
or for the eagles to fly,
or for the jet streams to lead the jets.

And everyone had to walk around with
flashlights so they could see.

But there was one little boy who said, "I am going to fix this." He started looking for the wolf who ate the sky.

But first he came upon a little mouse.
"Have you seen the wolf who ate the
sky? I am going to find him and get
the sky back."

The mouse said, "No, I haven't seen
him but that's a great idea. I'll come
along to help."

Soon they came upon a lion. "Have you seen the wolf who ate the sky? We are going to find him and get the sky back."

The lion said,
"No, I haven't
seen him but I
would love to help.
May I join you?"

"Of course," said the boy.

Then the three of them saw a campfire with lots of animals around it. There was a giraffe, a monkey, two squirrels, a dog, three bats, and many more. The boy spoke up and said, "Excuse me, but have any of you seen the wolf who ate the sky? We want to get the sky back."

All the creatures said, "No, we haven't seen him but that's a fine idea. Can we come too?"

The boy said, "Yes, that would be great."

Then all the creatures started walking together in one long line, looking for the wolf who ate the sky. Suddenly they heard a deep howl. "That's him!" cried the boy.

All the animals got very quiet and
made a plan. The boy led them and
they all crept carefully toward where
the howl came from.

Sure enough, there was the wolf
by a campfire.

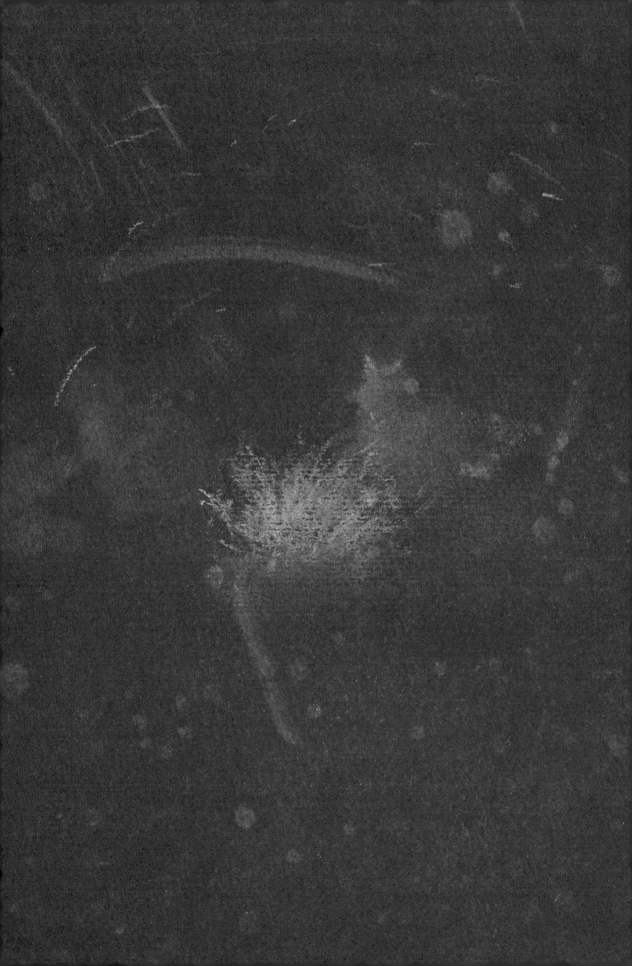

The big
animals, like the
lion and the giraffe,
made a commotion,
banging on trees and
making funny noises.

Surprised, the wolf opened his mouth wide in astonishment.

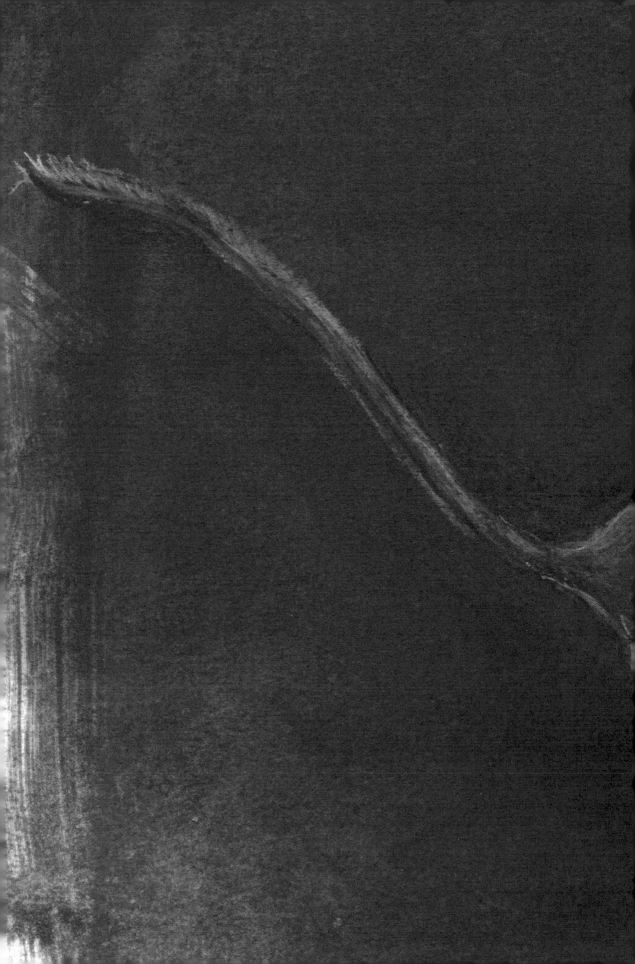

That was when the mouse jumped inside
the wolf's mouth and slid down his
throat to his belly, where the sky was
still shimmering.

The mouse grabbed a corner of the sky
and started pulling up.

"Help me!" she cried, and all the
animals came running. The squirrel
grabbed the mouse, and a dog grabbed
the squirrel, and all the animals made
a big long chain pulling on the sky.

They pulled
    and they pulled,
    and they pulled,
        and they pulled,
            and they pulled,
                and they pulled,

And then, "Pop!" The sky came out with a huge whoosh.

Like magic, light filled the world again.
And the sun could shine, and the
clouds could dance, and the eagles
could fly, and the jet streams could
lead the jets.

Then the animals all worked together and fed the wolf a big meal of oatmeal and raisins and nuts so that he would no longer be so hungry that he would eat the sky.

And just to be sure, the little boy climbed a ladder and screwed the sky to the ceiling of the world, so that no other wolf (or any other creature) could ever swallow it again.

Love the light in the world.
Feed the hungry.
Treasure working with friends.

Told and Retold

The Wolf Who Ate the Sky came into being as it was told and retold on several car trips to and from preschool when Anna was three years old. Anna would ask her mother to tell her a story. Her mother would ask, "About an animal?" and Anna would say, "Yes, tell me a story about a wolf." "And what about the wolf?" her mother would ask, and Anna would say, "He's a hungry wolf!"

Her mother then created a story using these details. The story really connected with Anna's imagination, and so later, Anna told her father the story. Then she told it to her grandfather and grandmother. She told it again and again in the car with her mother. Each time Anna retold the story, variations occurred. She would add a detail or change the animals. The story here is a distillation of the several versions. It was written down and edited by her mother, Mary Daniel Hobson, and then illustrated by her grandfather Charles Hobson. This story is shared here now as an inspiring example of how enriching it can be to co-create stories with children.

A video of Anna telling a version of the story can be seen at youtu.be/7EGU7IN46RQ.

About the Authors

A photographer from the age of fourteen, Mary Daniel Hobson works with mixed media to explore psychological geographies and the conflation of art and science. She enjoys sharing her creativity with her two young daughters. For more information, visit www.marydanielhobson.com.

Anna Rauh has loved storytelling, books, and reading since she was old enough to hold her first board books. It is this love of stories that inspired the co-creation of *The Wolf Who Ate the Sky* with her mother when she was three and a half years old.

Charles Hobson is a visual artist who explores the relationship between word and image in artists' books. He is an emeritus professor at the San Francisco Art Institute and his archive has been recently acquired by Stanford University. For more information, visit www.CharlesHobson.com.

Author photos by (top to bottom) Charles Hobson, Mary Daniel Hobson, and Alice Shaw

Library of Congress Cataloging-in-Publication Data
Hobson, Mary Daniel.
 The wolf who ate the sky / Mary Daniel Hobson and Anna Isabel Rauh ; images and design by Charles Hobson.
   pages cm
 Summary: A very hungry wolf eats the sky, plunging the whole world into darkness, but a brave boy and a menagerie of animals are determined to bring back the light. Includes author's note on how the story was developed with her three-year-old daughter, Anna, then illustrated by Anna's grandfather.
 ISBN 978-1-59714-298-4 (hardcover : alk. paper)
 [1. Sky--Fiction. 2. Wolves--Fiction. 3. Animals--Fiction.] I. Rauh, Anna Isabel. II. Hobson, Charles, 1943- illustrator. III. Title.
 PZ7.H637Wol 2015
 [E]--dc23
                    2014026475

Heyday is an independent, nonprofit publisher and unique cultural institution. We promote widespread awareness and celebration of California's many cultures, landscapes, and boundary-breaking ideas. Through our well-crafted books, public events, and innovative outreach programs we are building a vibrant community of readers, writers, and thinkers. To travel further into California, visit us at www.heydaybooks.com.

Cover Design: Ashley Ingram
Interior Design/Typesetting: Rebecca LeGates

Orders, inquiries, and correspondence should be addressed to:
Heyday
P.O. Box 9145, Berkeley, CA 94709
(510) 549-3564, Fax (510) 549-1889
www.heydaybooks.com

Printed in China by Imago

10 9 8 7 6 5 4 3 2 1